Toot & Puddle
A Present for Toot

by Holly Hobbie

Little, Brown and Company
Boston New York Toronto London

First Edition

Library of Congress Cataloging-in-Publication Data

Hobbie, Holly.
    Toot and Puddle : a present for Toot / by Holly Hobbie. — 1st ed.
        p.   cm.
    Summary: When he just about gives up trying to find the right birth-
day gift for Toot in Pip's Pet Shop, Puddle needs to look no further
because the special present finds him.
    ISBN 0-316-36556-4
    [1. Birthdays — Fiction.   2. Gifts — Fiction.]   I. Title.
PZ7.H6517 To   1998
[E] — dc21   97-15746

10 9 8 7 6 5 4 3 2 1

SC

Published simultaneously in Canada by Little, Brown & Company
(Canada) Limited

Printed in Hong Kong

The paintings for this book were done in watercolor. The text type was
set in Optima, and the display type was set in Windsor Light and Poetica.

For Hope

It was already Tuesday, and Toot's birthday was on Friday.
Puddle wanted to get him the best present ever.

"What do you want for your birthday?" Puddle asked.

"I don't need a thing," said Toot, who was busy bird-watching.

"Just tell me," Puddle pleaded.

"Surprise me," Toot said. He pointed. "A nuthatch!"

"Toot," Puddle said, "I'm serious."

"Okay," Toot said. "Anything."

Going shopping made Puddle nervous.

In the Blue Ox Bookstore, he saw many books he'd like, but he couldn't find the right book for Toot.

In Hardy's Hardware, Puddle fell in love with a red-handled hammer. . . .

In Ted's Sport Shop, his favorite thing was a big shiny bowling ball, but Toot had never liked bowling.

And he wanted everything in Kate's Kitchen Shop. But it's not Puddle's birthday, he reminded himself. It's Toot's birthday.

Puddle returned home empty-handed — and pooped out.

The next day Puddle slipped off to town again while Toot was
having breakfast. He spent all morning traipsing through stores.
Toot is special, he thought — that's the problem.

Puddle liked everything he saw in Pip's Pet Shop.

But Toot had traveled all over the world, Puddle considered.
He had seen *amazing* animals.
"Toot is too special for ordinary pets," he said aloud.

"Maybe," a strange voice said.

"Excuse me?" Puddle said.

"Excuse me," the voice said back.

"Hello?" Puddle said, looking around.

"Hello," repeated the voice.

"Are you talking to me?" Puddle asked.

THE
CAT

THE
DOG

Youn
1ST

"I think I am," said a parrot. "Toot is too special," it said, imitating Puddle. "Well, I'm no ordinary pet," the bird said. "You could say I'm *exotic*."

"What's your name?" Puddle asked.
"Tulip," said the parrot.
"I'm Puddle. What are you doing here?"

"I traveled here with a sailor friend," Tulip explained. "But I got tired of living on a ship, so he brought me to Pip's. I've been staying here since summer, and I'm getting pretty bored."
"Well, why don't you leave?" Puddle asked.
"I can't just leave," Tulip told him. "I need a place to live."

"I see," said Puddle.
"And I'm quite expensive," Tulip said.

Puddle couldn't stop thinking about Tulip. He had just enough money to buy an expensive pet. But was Tulip the right present? Then Puddle remembered the words Tulip had spoken: "I need a place to live."

On Thursday Toot and Puddle had a picnic brunch.
"Your birthday is almost here," Puddle said. "Isn't there one thing you want?"
"I thought you were going to surprise me," said Toot.
"Maybe I will."

"I hope you'll like living at Woodcock Pocket," Puddle said.

"I think I will," said Tulip.

"Since you're a surprise," Puddle said, "you'll have to hide in the toolshed. Just for tonight."

"I understand," said Tulip. "I'm getting butterflies."

"Me, too," said Puddle.

That night Toot was looking at his picture album of Africa.
"What kinds of birds did you see in Africa?" Puddle asked.
"All kinds," Toot said.

"What about parrots?" Puddle asked.
"I only saw one or two parrots," Toot replied, "but I heard them all the time."
"Really?"
"They screech and squawk like mad," Toot said. "We're lucky we don't have parrots around here."

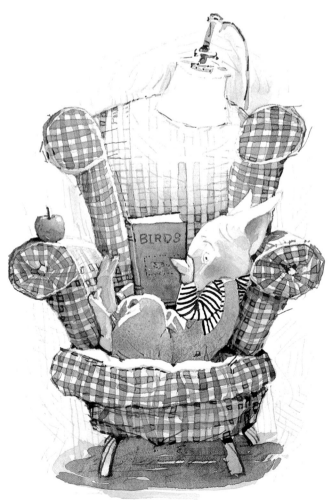

Puddle was afraid he had made a terrible mistake. His friend didn't want parrots around there. And if Tulip was unhappy at Woodcock Pocket, it would be Puddle's fault.
Poor Tulip, he thought.

"Tulip, where are you?" he called softly. His heart was pounding. "I'm freezing," said the parrot. She stuck her head out from under an old blanket. "You didn't tell me it would be so cold."

"Only for tonight," Puddle said. "It's warm in the house."
"It's pretty lonely, too," Tulip said. "Compared to Pip's Pet Shop."
"It's not at all lonely in the house," Puddle said. "But I'll keep you company out here tonight."

"Are you awake?" Puddle asked.

"Totally," Tulip said.

"I was thinking," said Puddle. "You don't have to stay at Woodcock Pocket if you don't want to."

Tulip didn't say anything.

"I mean," Puddle went on, "there are other places to live."

"I know *that*," Tulip said. She added, "I think I'll stay."

Friday came.

"You can't go in the toolshed," Puddle told Toot.

"All right," Toot said. He had a big smile on his pink face.

It's time to party, Puddle thought.

"Puddle, what in the world do you have on your head?"
Toot asked.
"Something special," Puddle said nervously.

"Surprise," Puddle said.
"Surprise," Tulip said.
"Who are you?" Toot asked.
"Well, it looks like I'm your present," said Tulip.

"And now," Tulip said, "*I* have a little something for Toot."
She reached around with her beak and plucked out one
bright red tail feather.

"Happy birthday!" she said.

Toot stared. "It's beautiful," he said. "Thank you." And he
stuck it in his favorite hat right away.

Puddle was just as surprised as Toot. "Didn't that hurt?"
he asked.

"It just pinched," said Tulip.

"Well, I guess that wasn't an ordinary birthday
with ordinary presents," Puddle said. "Was it?"
"It was extraordinary," Toot said.
"You could say *exotic*," said Tulip.